Jimmy Finnigan's WILD WOOD BAND

TOM KNIGHT

t

templar publishing

This is the village where Jimmy Finnigan lives.
Have you ever seen a nicer place?

The park was so nice that Mr Appleyard, the park keeper,
would not let anyone walk on the grass.

The police station was very nice too. And there was hardly any crime,
so Sergeant Marchant spent his time knitting jumpers for cats and dogs.

Jimmy's school was especially nice. And his teacher, Miss Primula,
was so nice that she even let the children come to school on Saturdays.

There was only one thing that wasn't nice about where Jimmy Finnigan lived,
and that was the woods. You wouldn't call them nice at all.

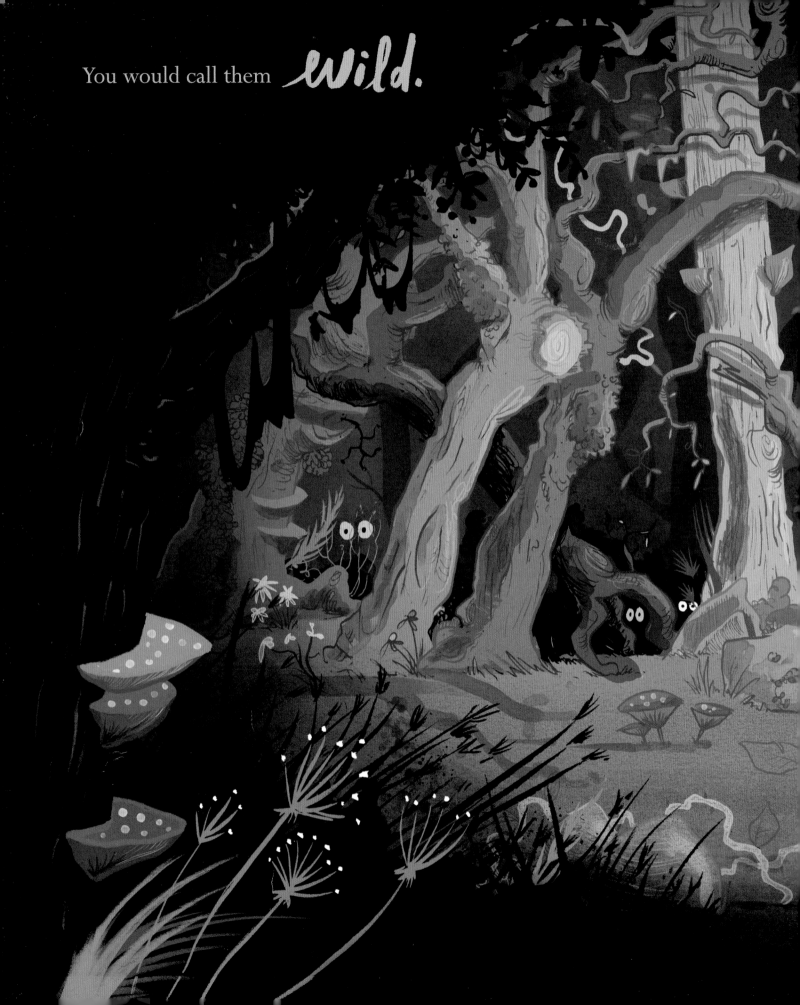

You would call them *wild.*

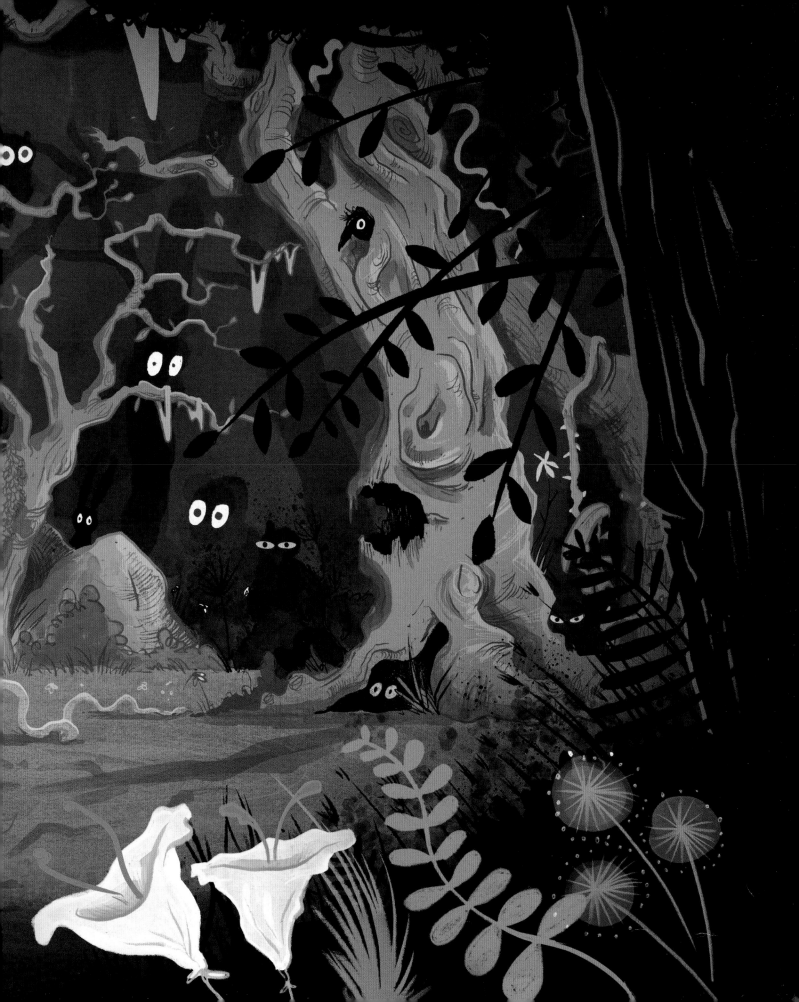

They were so wild that everyone from the village warned the children to stay away

Jimmy's mum and dad didn't want him going into the woods either.

But Jimmy found something quite different.

THE JANGLES

NOVEMBER 13TH
TOWNHOUSE
DOORS AT 8

VIP
ACCESS
ALL
AREAS

"Those are records,"
explained Dad. "It's how
people listened to music
in the olden days."
And he showed Jimmy
how to play one.

MUM + DAD'S

FRAGILE

First Jimmy's head started to bob.

Then his bottom started to wiggle.

Soon he was waving his arms about and jumping all over the place.

And soon . . .

. . . Jimmy Finnigan had started to play his own music.

Soon music was all Jimmy could think about.

He dreamed of forming his own band.

So he designed a poster . . .

But for some reason, nobody called.

Then Jimmy put a poster in the one place that everyone was always telling him not to go.

The next day, that had been taken down too.

Screamed Jimmy Finnigan.

Just then, Jimmy heard
a strange noise.

He started
to follow it.

His head
started to bob.

| His bottom started to wiggle. | His arms started to wave about. | And he started jumping all over the place. |

Suddenly Jimmy found himself standing in a clearing with three of the **Wildest** creatures he'd ever seen.

"We saw your poster,"
said the wolf.

"We want to join your band,"
said the beaver.

"We were just practising
to make sure we were
good enough,"
said the bear.

"Well, I think you sound AMAZING!" shouted Jimmy,
and he plugged in his guitar.

Meanwhile, in the village, loud noises were heard coming from the woods.

And so the villagers walked into the *wild* woods.

Finally, they stepped into the clearing.

First they froze.

Then they gawped.

But then their heads started to bob, their bottoms started to wiggle, their arms started to wave about, and they started to jump about all over the place.

By the time Jimmy and the band noticed the villagers were there, everyone was dancing. It was WILD.

After that, things were a bit different in Jimmy's village.

The school was different.

The police station was different . . .

. . . and the park was *very* different.

This is the village where Jimmy Finnigan lives.
It's still a really nice place to live,
but now it's just a little bit **WILD** too.

More picture books from Templar:

ISBN: 978-1-78370-418-7 (hardback)
978-1-78370-419-4 (paperback)

ISBN: 978-1-78370-386-9 (hardback)
978-1-78370-387-6 (paperback)

ISBN: 978-1-78370-389-0 (hardback)

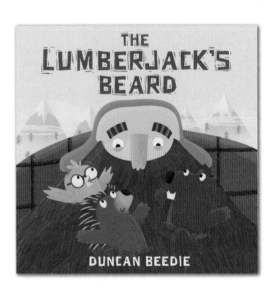

ISBN: 978-1-78370-687-7 (hardback)
978-1-78370-688-4 (paperback)

www.templarco.co.uk